Jill Dow trained at the Royal College of Art,
and specialises in illustrating children's books
about animals and natural history.
Her finely detailed artwork is based on
a love of nature and the countryside,
giving her illustrations rare charm and realism.
Her previous books include the
Bellamy's Changing World series,
(with writer and conservationist David Bellamy),
and the highly successful *Windy Edge Farm* stories,
which she has both written and illustrated.

Jill Dow lives in Thornhill, near Stirling, Scotland,
with her husband and their three young children.

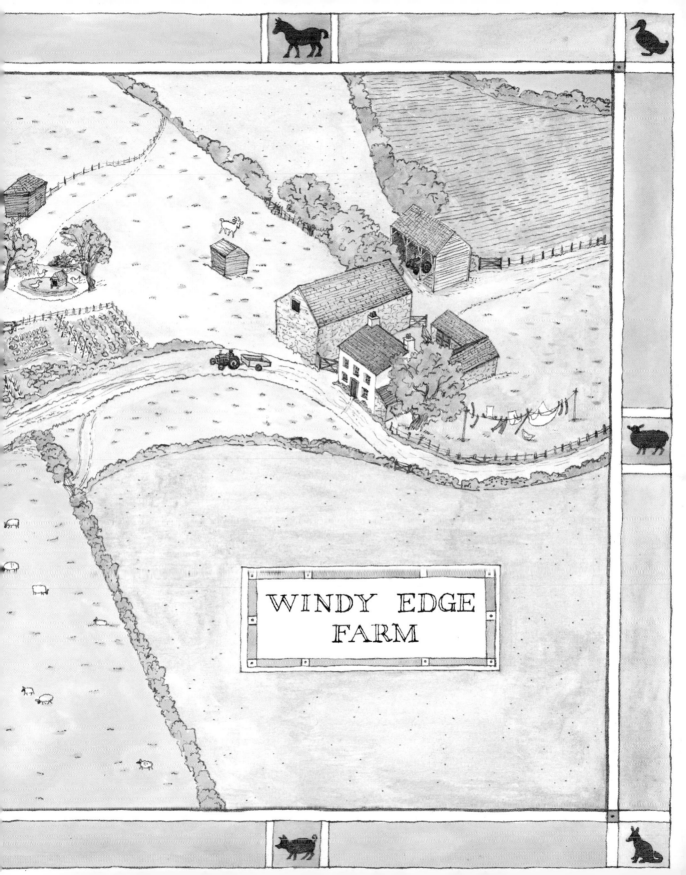

WINDY EDGE
FARM

For Joan, Amanda and Stacy

First published in Great Britain in 1994 by
Frances Lincoln Limited, 4 Torriano Mews
Torriano Avenue, London NW5 2RZ

British Library Cataloguing in Publication Data
available on request

ISBN 0-7112-0851-4-hardback
ISBN 0-7112-0852-2-paperback

Printed in Hong Kong

3 5 7 9 8 6 4 2

MAGGIE'S HOLIDAY

Jill Dow

FRANCES LINCOLN

Maggie was a pony who loved company. She was very happy living with Mr McNab, up the lane from Windy Edge Farm. He kept lots of other animals too – some cows and sheep, three goats, two donkeys, a dozen hens, and five white geese.

Maggie shared a field with the donkeys, next to Mr McNab's busy yard. There was always plenty for her to watch.

Maggie loved
children, and
so did Mr McNab.
They were always
pleased when Angus
came up from Windy Edge Farm. He usually
brought something tasty for Maggie, and often
helped to groom her and muck out her stable.

Sometimes Mr McNab hitched Maggie up to the pony trap, and off they all went. Maggie loved trotting along the lanes, up and down the hills, with the wind blowing in her long mane.

But Mr McNab was getting too old to look after all the animals. First he sold the donkeys and the goats, then the cows and sheep. He sold all the hens except for Mavis, who laid him one brown egg for breakfast every morning. And he gave the five white geese to Angus's mum.

"I wish we could take you home too," said Angus, stroking Maggie's velvety nose, "but Mum says we've already got enough animals at Windy Edge, and Mr McNab says he'll never part with you because you're his favourite."

Just before Christmas, Mr McNab decided
to visit his son in Australia. He asked Angus
to look after Maggie and Mavis while he was
away. Every morning, Angus came to feed
them and let them out before he rushed off
to school.

Maggie wished he could stay. She missed
Mr McNab, and her field was lonely without
the donkeys. It was quiet too: no cows mooing
or sheep bleating, no cockerels crowing or
geese hissing. With only Mavis to keep her
company, the short winter days seemed
very long.

After school, Angus came back at last. He fed Maggie and mucked out her stable, but he had to hurry home before dark.

Maggie was pleased when Angus's Christmas holidays began. Now he could stay much longer!

Sometimes Angus's mum came too. They put on
the pony's saddle and Maggie took Angus for
a ride.

"Oh, Maggie, I wish you could come and live
at Windy Edge Farm!" sighed Angus, as they
cantered round the field.

One night, a great storm blew up. Angus lay
awake listening to the wind whistling round
the chimney pots and rattling the roof. When he
looked out, all he could see was whirling snow.
He knew he was safe inside the farmhouse, but
would Maggie be safe in her rickety old stable?

The pony was listening to the gale too. Gust
after gust shook the stable, and flakes of icy
snow blew through all the cracks. Suddenly
a huge gust burst the door open, and the wind
rushed in and tore the roof off with a loud
R-R-R-Rip!

The blizzard finally died away, but poor Maggie was too cold to sleep. She huddled in a corner until the sun began to rise, then plodded out into the field. Mavis came stepping daintily across the snowdrifts to join her. The henhouse had lost its roof too, and the little hen was lucky not to have been blown away.

Together they went to the gate. If only Angus would come!

But Angus was still at Windy Edge Farm. The snow was so deep, the only way he could reach Maggie was to go on the tractor with Mr Finlay. First they had to dig the tractor out of a snowdrift!

At last Maggie and Mavis heard the rumble of
Mr Finlay's tractor struggling up the hill.
Maggie tossed her head and whinnied with
delight as Angus jumped down and waded
towards her through the deep snow.

The pony nuzzled her cold nose into his pocket to see what he had brought.

"Don't worry," Angus said. "We're going to take you back to Windy Edge Farm before another storm blows up!"

Mr Finlay found an old box for Mavis, and put her in the tractor. Angus trudged behind, leading Maggie along the tyre tracks. Maggie didn't know where she was going, but she knew she would be safe with Angus.

More snow began to fall as they set off down the hill. The wind howled and blew snow in their eyes. It seemed a very long way, but at last they arrived at Windy Edge Farm. Soon Maggie and Mavis were warm and cosy in the barn.

Next day was Christmas Day. Angus gave
Maggie a rosy red apple and showed her around
the farm. She recognised Mr McNab's five white
geese, and was especially pleased to meet some
new donkeys.

All week, the sun shone in a frosty sky, and
Maggie had fun with Angus in the snow.
She trotted round the field, watching as he
swooped down the hill on his new sledge.
The snow was so deep and soft, it didn't
matter if he fell off.

But on Friday night, it began to rain.
By morning, all the snow had melted,
leaving the lane covered in puddles and
the fields all soggy and wet. The holidays
were nearly over, and Angus felt gloomy.
He went to see Maggie and brushed her
until she shone like a horse chestnut.

"Oh Maggie," he sighed, "I *am* going to miss
you when Mr McNab comes back!"

Just then, Mr Finlay put his head round the
door. "Guess what, Angus! Mr McNab has
written from Australia. He likes it so much, he's
decided to stay there. And what do you think he
wants us to do with Maggie?"

"Does he want us to keep her?" Angus whispered.

His father nodded.

"Oh Dad," shouted Angus "Can we? Please?"

"Well, I suppose so," said Mr Finlay, smiling. "As long as you promise to help look after her."

Angus couldn't think of anything he'd like better, and neither could Maggie!

– The End –

OTHER **WINDY EDGE FARM** PAPERBACKS

BRIDGET'S SECRET
Every day Bridget the hen lays her egg in a special place,
and Angus has to search for it. One day
Angus can't find the egg anywhere - nor can he find Bridget. . .
ISBN 0-7112-0570-1 £4.99

MOLLY'S SUPPER
Molly the cat stays out on the farm all day, and when evening comes
she is far away. Will Molly get home in time to be fed?
ISBN 0-7112-0569-8 £3.50

HEPZIBAH'S WOOLLY FLEECE
When the wind blows Hepzibah into a prickly bush, she has to wait
until she is rescued - and she wishes her woolly fleece were not so long. . .
ISBN 0-7112-0616-3 £2.95

WEBSTER'S WALK
Webster the duck takes all the other farmyard ducks on a walk to the river.
They are happy among the wild river birds until a storm suddenly comes. . .
ISBN 0-7112-0614-7 £4.99

PIGGY LITTLE'S HIDE & SEEK
When all the piglets escape, Angus can't find the littlest one.
He looks and looks: where on earth can Piggy Little be?
ISBN 0-7112-0730-5 £3.50

HAZEL & CLOVER'S GREAT ESCAPE
Hazel and Clover, the two white goats, are determined to escape
from their field and have some fun. This means trouble for everyone. . .
ISBN 0-7112-0732-1 £3.99

MOONBEAM'S BIG SPLASH
Moonbeam the calf decides to go exploring. What happens next,
and how Angus comes to her rescue, make perfect bedtime reading.
ISBN 0-7112-1028-4 £4.99

Windy Edge Farm books are suitable for National Curriculum English - Reading, Key Stage 1
Scottish Guidelines English Language - Reading, Level B

Frances Lincoln titles are available at all good bookshops.
Prices are correct at time of printing, but may be subject to change.